CONTENTS

THE TOUCH OF BHASMASURA

Long ago, demon King Bhasmasura concentrated hard on praying to Lord Shiva.

Ultimately, his prayers were answered. Lord Shiva appeared and said, "Tell me, what is it you want, Bhasmasura?"

Bhasmasura immediately demanded, "Give me such power that if I touch anyone's head; man, god or demon, with my right hand, he would be reduced to a heap of ashes!"

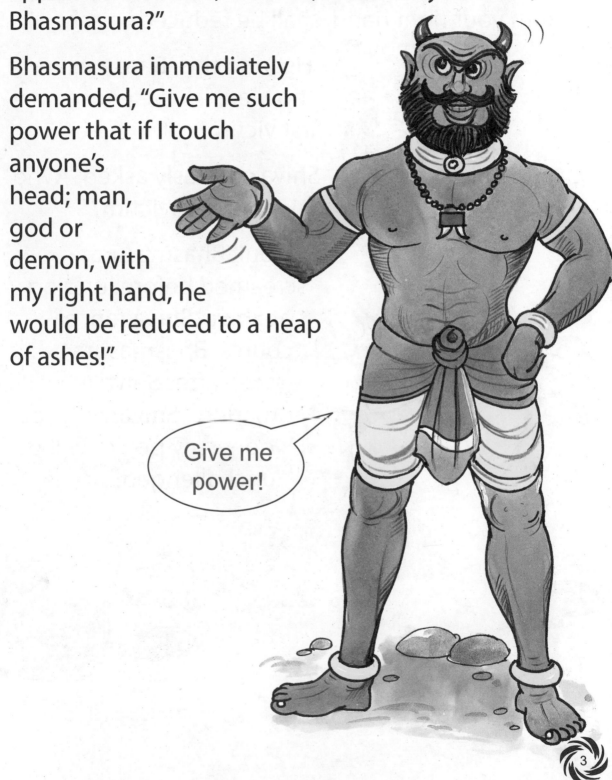

Give me power!

Lord Shiva solemnly declared, "I grant you this boon. Whoever you touch, man, god or demon, with your right hand, shall be reduced to ashes!"

Hearing this, Bhasmasura howled, "I have chosen my first victim."

Shiva curiously asked, "Who is your first victim?"

"You!" Bhasmasura screamed before lunging at Shiva. Shiva ran, of course. Bhasmasura raced after Shiva, roaring, "Shiva with you gone, my power will be unchallenged!"

To Shiva's dismay, Bhasmasura chased him closely. "Vishnu, Vishnu!" Shiva called his friend desperately. Bhasmasura gave Shiva no respite! "Vishnuuuuuu!" Shiva desperately shouted.

Shiva took a five-step advance and lost Bhasmasura for spilt seconds. By now, Lord Vishnu had arrived. Vishnu was very amused. Shiva hysterically cried, "Don't just stand there smiling. Do something, Vishnu!"

"Go behind the mountain and wait,"Vishnu instructed. "Come on out, Shiva," Bhasmasura yelled. Of course, Shiva did not appear. But someone else did.

A striking, beautiful woman, swirled out. Bhasmasura stood stunned.

She circled gracefully around the demon. On seeing her, Bhasmasura's cruel expression was replaced by a love sick one.

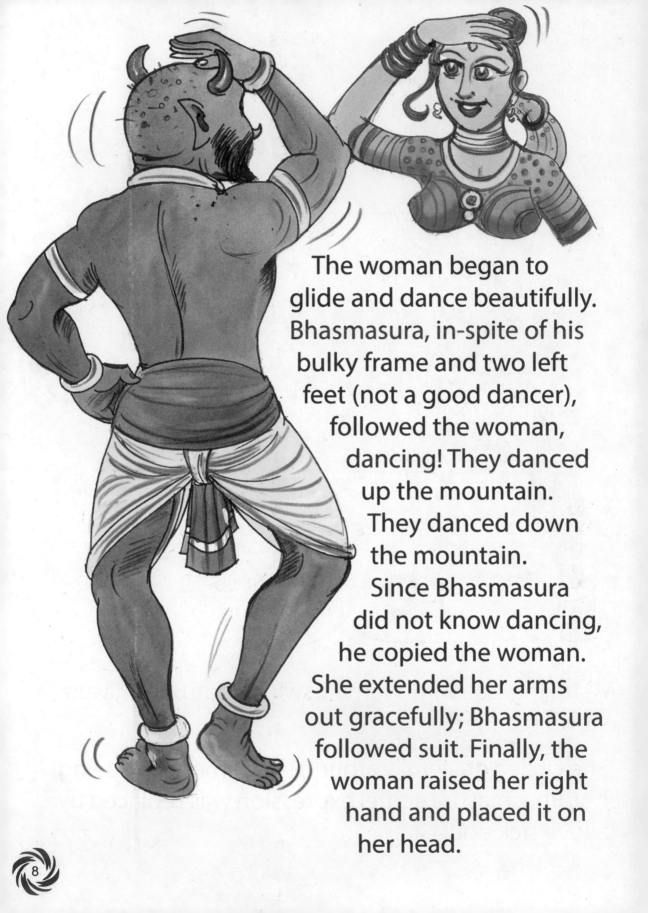

The woman began to glide and dance beautifully. Bhasmasura, in-spite of his bulky frame and two left feet (not a good dancer), followed the woman, dancing! They danced up the mountain. They danced down the mountain. Since Bhasmasura did not know dancing, he copied the woman. She extended her arms out gracefully; Bhasmasura followed suit. Finally, the woman raised her right hand and placed it on her head.

Bhasmasura, with half shut eyes, copied her.

"Whoooooooooosh!" He had touched his own head!

Just as Shiva had ordained: "Bhasmasura, whoever you touch, god, man or demon, shall turn to ashes."

Within fractions of seconds, Bhasmasura was a heap of ashes. Suddenly, a transformation began and the woman changed into Lord Vishnu. Yes, the woman was Mohini. A guise Vishnu often used to trick enemies.

"Thank you Vishnu," Lord Shiva said, coming out from behind the mountain.

Think before you speak.

HARISHCHANDRA

King Harishchandra was a pious, charitable and honest king. "I do not believe that Harishchandra is that truthful. Let us see how honest and truthful he actually is in adverse times," Lord Indra challenged.

Sage Vishwamitra agreed to help Indra in this plot. To fullfill this plan, Vishwamitra appeared in Harishchandra's dreams.

In his dream, Harishchandra saw Vishwamitra asking him for his entire kingdom.

"My kingdom is yours, holy sage!" Harishchandra observed himself saying.

To Harishchandra's horror, the next morning, Vishwamitra arrived at the courts.

"Give me your kingdom, Harishchandra. You promised me in your dream last night that your kingdom is mine," Vishwamitra roared. Harishchandra promptly handed over his entire kingdom to Vishwamitra! Harishchandra himself retired to Kashi.

This was the only place that was not included in the kingdom. But Vishwamitra still wanted more.

"You, as a king, claim to be charitable? If you are true to your words, give me charity." Harishchandra sold his wife and child as house help to a Brahmin. He then handed the money he got for them to the sage.

Vishwamitra refused to accept Harishchandra's small offering.

King Harishchandra took up a job at a cremation ground. This way he paid the sage more charity. One day, Harishchandra's wife discovered their son had died from a snakebite. At the cremation ground, she met her husband. Harishchandra still did not forget the rules of his job.

"Please pay me," said he. Helplessly, his wife tore one part of her threadbare sari and offered it to him. Accepting this as payment, Harishchandra began to prepare for the funeral. A blinding light stopped him.

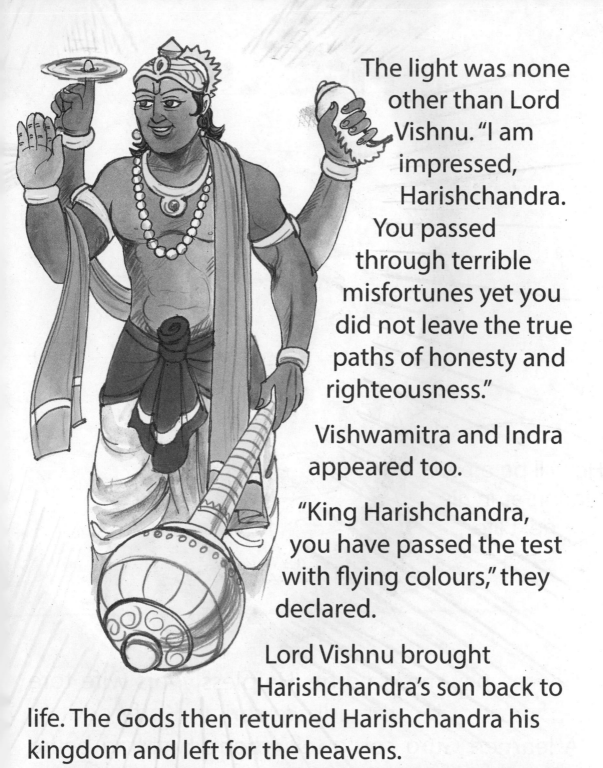

The light was none other than Lord Vishnu. "I am impressed, Harishchandra. You passed through terrible misfortunes yet you did not leave the true paths of honesty and righteousness."

Vishwamitra and Indra appeared too.

"King Harishchandra, you have passed the test with flying colours," they declared.

Lord Vishnu brought Harishchandra's son back to life. The Gods then returned Harishchandra his kingdom and left for the heavens.

Stand by your principles, come what may.

In the end, triumph will be yours.

A PIG'S LIFE

He will be a poor labourer in his next life

A learned Guru could tell what any living being would be reborn after death. When he saw the rich merchant, he could foresee that he would be reborn as a poor worker in his next birth.

'I am going to be reborn as a pig,' the Guru brooded. He did not quite like that. "I must do something about it," decided the Guru.

"Shishya (student), I have a duty for you," the Guru addressed his most devoted disciple.

"Observe this birthmark on my forehead closely. I have come to know, with my vested powers, that I am going to die very soon."

"Oh no! Do not say that," the disciple cried.

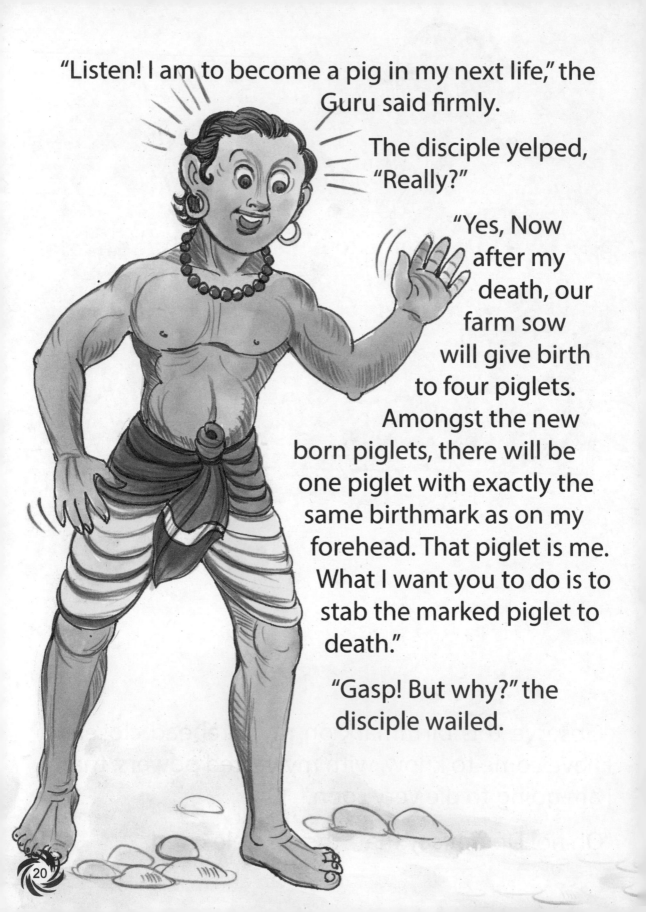

"Listen! I am to become a pig in my next life," the Guru said firmly.

The disciple yelped, "Really?"

"Yes, Now after my death, our farm sow will give birth to four piglets. Amongst the new born piglets, there will be one piglet with exactly the same birthmark as on my forehead. That piglet is me. What I want you to do is to stab the marked piglet to death."

"Gasp! But why?" the disciple wailed.

The Guru explained, "That way, I'll be immediately released from a pig's life. I will be reborn to a better life thereon." This made sense to the disciple. He said, "I will do as you say."

A few months later, the Guru fell grievously ill and died. One day, it came to be known that the farm sow was about to have piglets.

Soon, four piglets were born. The disciple immediately identified a fat piglet smudged with a bright birthmark.

The disciple ran inside to get a sharp knife. He raised the knife to stab the piglet, just as the Guru had instructed. Suddenly, the piglet shrieked in a human voice, "No! Stop! Don't kill me!"
The disciple was taken aback.

No! Stop! Don't kill me

The piglet said, "Now that I'm here, I like it. This mud is comfortable. I nestle close to my loving mother who feeds me delicious milk."

The disciple lowered the knife and did not kill the piglet. Later, the disciple brought the piglet home and raised it with loving care. He often thought, 'Imagine, this pig was my Guru in his previous birth. I know that so I care for it with such passion. Maybe if everyone knew this, they would treat animals more kindly.'

Respect and love all living beings.

FOREIGNER'S PRIVILEGE

Many, many years ago, an Afghan Pathan crossed the borders and came into India.

At a sweetmeat shop, he mis-understood the word 'Khaja.' He asked the seller what the name of the sweet was and the seller said "Khaja".

Thinking he meant 'eat'- the foreigner ate and ate not realizing that 'khaja' had two meanings! One meaning is to 'eat' and it was also the name of a sweet meat. After eating, he simply left. "Hey, wait! Give me the money," demanded the sweet meat seller. The foreigner ignored him and kept walking.

"Stop, thief," yelled the seller. This shout alarmed a policeman who raced towards the foreigner. He soon caught up with the Pathan.

"Pay for the sweets," snarled the constable. The Pathan did not understand a word of what the constable was saying. So, the foreigner just smiled, shaking his head.

The policeman grabbed the Pathan's hand, shouting, "You are under arrest."

The Pathan smiled, thinking, 'This man is probably inviting me to his home.' The policeman marched the foreigner off to the police station. "In our town, stealing is a great offence so you will be punished accordingly," babbled the policeman.

The Pathan did not understand a word. He assumed that the policeman was trying to welcome him.

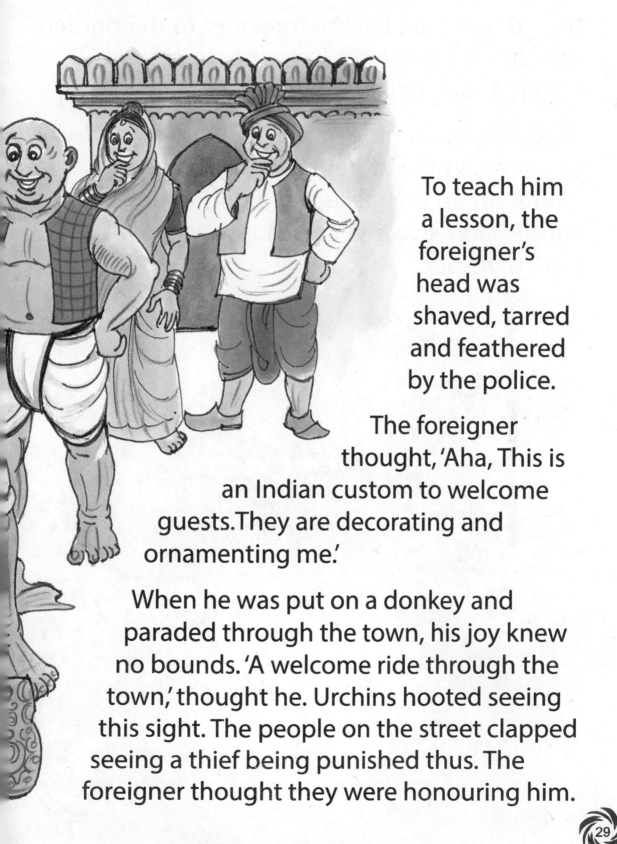

To teach him a lesson, the foreigner's head was shaved, tarred and feathered by the police.

The foreigner thought, 'Aha, This is an Indian custom to welcome guests.They are decorating and ornamenting me.'

When he was put on a donkey and paraded through the town, his joy knew no bounds. 'A welcome ride through the town,' thought he. Urchins hooted seeing this sight. The people on the street clapped seeing a thief being punished thus. The foreigner thought they were honouring him.

The donkey man led the foreigner to the borders and waved a good-bye. Once home, he told all his friends about India.

"Magnificent country," he exclaimed, "you can point to sweets in the street and they give you some for free. Then they take you along to one of their houses, and shave your head, which is a special mark of respect.

They anoint your head with warm, soothing ointment. Then they honour their visitors with a ceremonial ride through the town on a donkey. I shall always remember the kindness I received there. My only regret is that I should have filled my bag with those delicious sweets. Then you could all taste them too!"

Ignorance is bliss.

THE RIDDLE

One day, emperor Akbar decided to ask his courtiers a riddle.

He went towards the palace wall and drew a line with a piece of chalk on the bare wall. "Now make this line, which I have drawn, shorter. But you can only do so without touching it," Akbar pompously ordered. Not one of the courtiers could solve this baffling riddle.

When told what the commotion was about, Birbal calmly walked to the Emperor and requested, "May I have the chalk please." Akbar gave the chalk piece to Birbal.

Ha, ha, you are all fools!

Birbal went towards the wall and drew a line parallel to the one Akbar had made. But Birbal made his line longer than the one Akbar had already marked on the wall. "Sire, now since my line is longer, your line has been shortened without being touched!" Akbar's mouth was wide open in amazement. He had once again been out-witted by the clever Birbal. Chuckling loudly, Akbar acknowledged defeat.

Now your line is shorter

Common sense is not common to everyone.

THE QUARRELLING OTTERS

Deep inside a jungle, in a cave, lived a jackal with his family. One day, his wife asked him to get fish for dinner.

But the Jackal was terrified of the fast moving waters of the river. As he neared the river, he saw two otters sitting on a rock. Just then, one otter dived into the water and held a fish by its tail. The fish was very big and the otter was struggling to hold on to it.

The second otter plunged into the water. Together, the two otters overpowered the struggling fish and brought it to the river-bank.

"Come, let's divide it."

"Yes, I'll take two-thirds and you take the rest."

"Why are you taking a bigger portion?" said the second otter sharply.

"I caught it, didn't I?" retorted the first otter glaring at the second one. "

"How dare you?" cried the first otter and smacked the second one. The jackal cleared his throat. "Friends, why are you quarrelling?"

"We are unable to divide the fish. Kindly help us," said the otters. "Very well," agreed the jackal. The jackal divided the fish into three pieces. He tossed the head portion to the first otter and the tail portion to the second otter. "The middle portion is my fee for settling your quarrel," said the jackal.

The jackal, with the fish, swiftly ran back to his wife. Crestfallen, the otters stared at the bony fish portions and said, "It was very foolish of us to have quarrelled. But for it, we would have been feasting on that plump fish instead of that jackal."

When friends fight, outsiders take advantage.